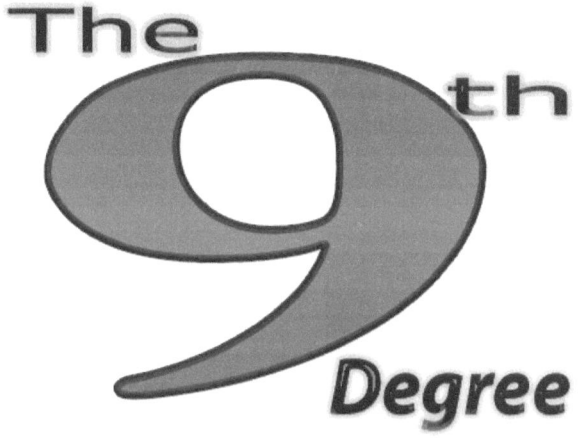

The 9th Degree

"Alex get's his five minutes of fame!"

Eric K. Williams Sr.

DEDICATION

I would like to thank my many friends and family who supported me in the creation of this book. This book gave true friends and loving family an opportunity to give support by providing feedback to this book.

My friend, Brian Culbertson, passed a few months after the first round of books edits. He offered helpful ideas and comments to provide motivation to move forward and weather the storm. I am stronger and better because of our friendship.

CONTENTS

ACKNOWLEDGMENTS

This book was an outlet for situations that seemed hard at the time. The time I spent creating this book allowed me to focus on the good things in life and not the people who decided to rain negativity because they had the power.

I would like to acknowledge my grandson, Gallo, who passed on to heaven after only a few months on this earth. I would just like to say that I love and miss him!

The proceeds from this book will go to local faith-based charities to provide for those who are in need of a helping hand.

Chapter 1

Beware Of The Changes You Make

The story begins with Alex who is a typical guy by all definitions. Since there is no exact definition for "normal", take this statement for what it's worth. He has a lot of great personal qualities, but his work colleagues only judge him by his one defining shortfall. He is considered an outcast at work because he cannot control his inner gases from flowing out of his body at certain critical times.

Elevators really amplify this urge because of the up and down motion combined with soft music. Elevators have always driven Alex crazy. Something about the atmosphere in an elevator continually throws his body into a state of uncontrollable hysteria. This hysteria is much like being uptight about some family drama you are trying to avoid while your favorite song is playing in the background on the radio. This situation gives him the urge to move his body to the beat. This action is uncontrollable, even though, yes, he knows dancing is not appropriate for the situation. Still, he cannot stop the feelings from flowing through his body. Alex has tried countless methods to control this problem but has been unsuccessful in finding even one way to prevent or curb his gaseous affliction

Always seeking a solution; Alex developed a friendship with Mr. J, the local transient celebrity whom he makes a point to converse with twice a week. Mr. J is well known throughout the city for being a talented consultant, philosopher, and even a prophet. The man's advice is always sane, witty, and easily understood. His unique method of communication utilized colorful stories, fluid motions, as well as musical references to provide solutions to just about any question asked. Mr. J survives by charging a fee for his services, usually some spare change.

Alex was having a terrible day, so be decided to go spend some time with his colorful friend. During a somber moment, Alex mentioned his elevator problem to Mr. J. The transient's response was to break out in a little song and dance. While singing "*Poppa gotta a brand-new bag.*", Mr. J stopped suddenly in a contorted pose as if someone pushed the pause button on a remote control. Alex could see he was earnest about helping fix this problem. M. J took great care in ensuring that Alex understood the words that were going to come out of his mouth. He pulled Alex close and whispered "*Follow these instructions to release your problems. I am warning you there may be evil forces looking to attack you for this high-level G-4 classified secret.*"

Mr. J. whispered a set of instructions to Alex like he was in a spy movie. Alex was eagerly paying attention to each step. Listening to the full set of instructions Alex felt that his advice was worth trying. Alex dug into his pocket and gave Mr. J three wrinkled greenbacks. He thought to himself, "The instructions were strange but, hell, they could help this situation or rectify the problem." Mr. J had emphasized that he follows his instructions to the letter, or the situation could end in tragedy. The rest of the day, Alex went to various stores collecting the articles and supplies as instructed. When Alex was finished, be headed to his apartment to start his quest.

Alex entered his apartment and quickly went to work on the instructions provided by his "*Loco*" transient friend. Alex took the largest Vidalia onion he could find and placed it in the microwave. He nuked it until he could see the outer layers of the onion pulsate. He used two handmade oven mitts of aluminum foil to rip the sweet pulsating onion out of the depths of the microwave. He quickly placed it in a bath of cold water and ice to shock it into releasing the evil that makes the onion bring tears to the eyes of people all over the world. He covered the bath of cold ice water with a red towel. Alex sang "*I got you babe*" for three minutes while "caressing the onion's soul in his mind", as Mr. J instructed.

Alex removed the handmade oven mitts and ripped the towel off the onion's cold bath of ice water. Quickly grabbing the onion, Alex placed it in the nearby blender with his bare hands. Mr. J explained that this action was to soothe the onion--to allow Alex to become linked with its evil empty soul. Alex pulled the onion back out of the blender. He took two steps back and shot the onion back into the blender like it was a basketball. He added a double dose of anti-gas pills and brewed a strong pot of coffee. The coffee needed to sit for 24 hours. The day-old coffee had to smell similar to *"something that would peel the paint off. "*

The next-day Alex tasted the concoction at precisely the 24-hour mark. The coffee tasted like somebody slapped the taste out of his mouth but smelled like his armpits after he had worked out at the gym. He added salt and pepper to produce a delicate balance to the rancid concoction. He poured five cups of the coffee in the blender with the onion and blended the mixture for exactly four minutes. He then picked up the blender's glass pitcher from the motor and shook it by hand for precisely three minutes. Next, he stirred the mixture with a wooden spoon for two exact minutes, poured it into three small ice trays, finally freezing the concoction into small bite size ice cubes for easy consumption. Alex realized that, though simple, Mr. J's instructions were a lot of work. He was in a state of exhaustion and quickly performed his nightly routine--sh*t, shower and shave, and laid down on his couch. He could hear the television infomercials playing as he dozed off into a deep sleep.

Alex woke up singing Jack LaLanne's theme song and immediately wanted to purchase a *"Sham Wow!"* Alex cleared his mind and quickly entered the kitchen. He opened the freezer and grabbed one of the small ice trays. He popped out a single cube, poured a cup of the two-day-old coffee, and gingerly washed a bowl of fresh strawberries. Alex began following Mr. J's second set of instructions, which, at this point, were complex in nature. Mr. J instructed him to take one frozen bite-size cube and stick it under his tongue. He was to sip the two-day-old coffee and eat each strawberry with the stem attached. Mr. J made a point to let Alex know that he had to sip the coffee and eat the strawberries until the bite-sized ice cube dissolved in his mouth. Alex could hear Mr. J saying, "*Keep your pinky down as your sip your troubles away!*"

The process was painful since the cold of the ice was sitting under the sensitive part of his tongue. The first couple of sips gave Alex a brain freeze. He could bear Mr. J saying, "*Brain freeze should not be a problem. Close your mouth and quit letting the cold in your head!*" Alex gritted his teeth in pain but kept following the instructions to the letter. The strong coffee taste, mixed with fresh strawberries, made the process barely palatable. Alex pushed all negative thoughts to the back of his mind. Still, he knew this concoction would probably fill the building with a scent so foul it would make him puke.

Alex finished the first batch of concoction and made a beeline to the bathroom to brush his teeth and rinse his mouth with cotton balls in his cheeks. Yes, Cotton Balls! Alex could hear Mr. J saying, "*Just because your butt smokes is no reason for your breath to be hot.*" He thought to himself "*Really! A smoking butt.*" Alex put on some fresh clothes and headed out the door of his apartment. His commute to the office went quickly with no delays.

Alex entered the first-floor lobby area of his office and waited for the elevator. This was easy to accomplish because none of his colleagues would ride the elevator with him. Alex entered the elevator, and after a few seconds, the urge to pass gas was so strong he began to squirm. He waited as long as he could, held his breath, and then slowly released his gas into the enclosed elevator space. Alex paused in anticipation of the ever-so-foul scent to waft from his trousers and fill the enclosed space of the elevator. He cautiously inhaled through his nose with a wrinkled expression on his face. Alex was pleasantly surprised when he could only smell the subtle scent of fresh strawberries.

The doors to the elevator gently slid open exposing the

outer world. The ride was over, and Alex slowly exited the elevator hoping to experience the subtle fresh strawberry scent as long as possible. Alex felt no emotion because he could not figure out how to feel. He strolled into his workspace with a feeling of numbness all over his body. He worked through lunch not even stopping for his customary stroll by the water cooler to hear the latest office gossip. The numbness in his heart turned into excitement as the workday came to a close.

Alex exited the building using the stairwell wanting to avoid the elevator at all costs. Alex had a clear mind as he drove straight home. He knew in his heart his life was going to be different. Alex set his sights on perfecting Mr. J's flatulation formula. Alex knew he needed to take a few days to make a plan that would fix his reputation. He knew rushing into a unique situation required precise planning and execution. This new revelation was going to help him gain much-needed popularity among his office colleagues.

The next couple of days, Alex tested the formula. He paid close attention to each experiment to ensure every detail led to perfection. Three days later, he entered the first-floor lobby and realized the five elevators were out of service for maintenance. Alex was left with no choice but to board the one good contraption with his work colleagues. The elevator was packed to capacity since it was the only one operating. Three of his colleagues who entered the elevator with Alex knew of his condition.

In the past, Alex would use his flatulating condition to get back at those colleagues who had backstabbed him in the office. Sometimes innocent employees would get caught in the elevator. The disappointment of having to ride with Alex had already set in. As he entered with his colleagues, they were displaying their disgust in anticipation of what was to come.

The doors closed, and the elevator began the motion that Alex always tried to handle but was never successful. He squirmed as all of his colleagues watched his many facial expressions; eventually he had no choice. Alex was unable to hold it. With all his strength, he stiffened the muscles of his gluteus maximus and turned to face the doors. He held on as long as he could, but he could feel his insides filling up with gas. He thought *"This is the Mother Load!"*. Were he to hold it any longer, it would probably come out of his mouth. Alex let himself relax and let one go steady, silent, and slow. His colleagues showed their anticipation by covering their noses and pumping their fists at him with their free hand.

Alex turned around to face his colleagues. Stella, his most vocal enemy, opened her eyes, and muttered, "Does anyone smell that? I think that is fresh strawberries and stale air." Disbelief on their faces, the others uncovered their noses and, taking a deep whiff confirmed the scent was, indeed, strawberries. The doors opened, and it seemed evident that no one wanted to exit the elevator. Alex did not move but stood straight and tall because this was his moment to shine.

The elevator doors began to close, and quite suddenly, Stella reached out and stopped the doors from closing. Using soft subtle movements, she gently pushed Alex out of the elevator. She let Alex know she was sorry, but he could not hold up everyone from getting to the office. The rest of his colleagues exited the elevator wondering what just happened.

During the day, word spread about his new talent. Alex decided to take the stairs for the next couple of days as office gossip circulated among his colleagues. He could tell that the office gossip channel was buzzing. Alex could not get anyone to give him the information about what was being said behind his back.

The weekend came, and Alex decided to spend his time experimenting with the formula. He let his imagination determine what his next move would be. He knew he needed to get it right to deflect the information being said in the gossip channel.

Monday morning he arrived at work early and found Stella waiting with six other people in the lobby. They invited Alex on the elevator first, then piled in after him giggling with anticipation. The doors closed, and Alex announced he had a special treat for the riders. A sense of excitement was in the air. All eyes were fixed on Alex hoping he could reproduce the previous subtitle strawberry scent.

Alex leaned back on the elevator wall and raised one foot 10 inches, releasing a light dose of silent but deadly gas that permeated the enclosed elevators space. Silence fell upon the elevator as his colleagues awaited the scent of strawberries.

Alex heard someone whisper softly *"That's smells like waffles and butter with Mrs. Butterworth's Syrup."* The crowd on the elevator seemed mesmerized by the scent. There was a pause as Alex raised his foot 5 more inches. Alex could hear two of his colleagues whisper *"The smell is changing! Is that considered a flavor shift?"* Once again, all eyes were on Alex, and he had a smile on his face that went from ear to ear.

Alex cleared his throat and announced to the crowd the flavor shift would be champagne with fresh peaches. The group closed their eyes and took a long sniff as if they were a synchronized swim team. Smiles came over everyone's face as the elevator reached the 10th floor, and the doors opened. Alex confirmed he was done with a simple nod and his colleagues left the elevator praising Alex for such an intense and flavorful experience.

The next few days, he provided elevator riders with a variety of scented experiences. In time, Stella became interested in Alex on a personal level. She would discreetly flirt with him by leaving sticky notes on his desk. During office lunch breaks, she would follow Alex into the stairwell, and eventually convinced him to let her come to his apartment. She wanted to help develop some of his scents by providing a woman's touch to his elevator experiences.

Alex had never been in a relationship with a girl longer than a couple of days. Stella was the first to show interest in him since the last girl who used to live in his apartment building. When she was drunk, his neighbor mistook him as her high school sweetheart. There were nights when she would knock on his apartment door, and when Alex would open the door, she would say, *"Harvey, are your parents asleep?"* Before Alex could respond, she would make her way to the couch, take off her heels, and make out with him. She would fall into a deep sleep after a few minutes.

Alex would let her sleep for a while until her loud snoring would begin to keep him up during the night. He would have to find a way to sneak her out of his apartment, take her down to the lobby, and leave her on one of the couches. Alex was never seen moving the drunken woman through the halls of the apartment building. Sometimes she would find her way back for a second siesta on his couch.

Alex did not mind because he was a good person. He knows that being a gentleman would pay off in the future. His dad was married to a wonderful woman and he knew one day he would have a loving relationship like his parents. He knew he had to be patient and let love come to him.

As the days passed the number of people waiting for him in the lobby began to decline as the novelty of his unusual talent wore off. One day, Alex noticed a few men hanging around the lobby elevators that were not a part of his office. One man always wore purple leg warmers, and the others wore scarves and stylish belts. The outfits were always meticulously coordinated with the rainbow theme. There was something different about these men, but he just could not put his finger on it.

The next day, Alex entered the lobby and noticed none of his fans were in the lobby, but the same four men from the previous day were there. Each dressed like they had just fallen out of a Skittles candy bag. Alex entered the elevator, and just as the doors began to close, an arm thrust through the door and the elevator doors opened. The five men entered, one at a time, as if to get their moment on the modeling runway. As the elevator doors closed, four of the men suddenly pushed Alex to the rear of the elevator, subduing him. The man in the purple leg warmers got right up in his face and asked him for his secret to pass scented flatulence.

Alex panicked, his mind began racing a million miles a

second. He opened his mouth but could not speak. The man in the purple leg warmers shouted, *"Spin and Spread!"* The four men spun Alex around in perfect sequence and gently spread his arms and legs slowly so as not to hurt him. The purple leg warmer man leaned over his shoulder and whispered in a soft gentle voice *"Tell me the secret, so we can let you go!"*

Alex panicked, and gas began to pour out of his backside. A loud clap sounded, as if lightning were in the closed elevator space. The clap was followed by rolling thunder that seemed to last an extended amount of time. Silence came to the elevator with a soft hissing sound slowly creeping out of the crease of his pants. The man in the purple leg warmers was still holding Alex's the belt loop. He tugged two times gently to get them open with a blank expression on his face.

The five men panicked and became motionless inside the elevator. Alex could hear them whispering to each other. He could hear them say, *"I smell flowers."* He heard the man in the purple leg warmers say, *"It's the fragrant but delectable scent of Cherry-Blossom Flowers."* The men began to dance in perfect harmony as the scent engulfed the closed elevator space. Four of the men were prancing in a circular motion. Alex could tell the man in purple leg warmers was fighting the urge to prance with the metro men. He simply tapped his foot and crossed his arms to hold his prancing urges in check. Suddenly, he stopped tapping his foot and uncrossed his arms. The scent was gradually changing in the enclosed elevator space. The man in the purple leg warmers stood on the tips of his toes and said: *"We are in the middle of a flavor shift, and it is going to be intense!"*

Alex's mind drifted to last night as Stella started their special time together by feeding him petals of Cherry-Blossom flowers and kissing him passionately. She jumped off of his lap and ran to the refrigerator. Stella grabbed a small bowl and returned slowly and sensually rubbing his chest as she wrapped her legs around his waist. Alex could not tell what was in the container.

Stella was panting heavily as she slid back into his lap.

Stella pulled him so close he could feel her beating heart and smell her soft, sweet-smelling perfume. She reached into the bowl and pushed a Jalapeno pepper into his mouth as she scratched his chest with her nails. This painful but seductive action caused him to chew and swallow the pepper without pain or heat.

This impulsive action by Stella placed Alex in a deep state of ecstasy. Her final act of passion happened as she violently pulls his hair back to open his mouth. She gazed into his eyes and stuffed a Habanero chili pepper into his mouth. She screamed, "*Swallow this one quickly!*" Once he began to swallow, she began to lick his lips with her tongue. She jumped off his lap and ran out of his apartment screaming "*You will thank me later.*"

Alex suddenly came back to reality. The four metro men stopped dancing because it was getting hot in the elevator. The Metro Men were too stylishly dressed to loosen or take off any clothes. Alex knew the heat from the Jalapeno peppers was going to make the room unbearable. Alex feared this would be the worst scent he had produced and did his best to get as close to the floor of the elevator as he could. The basic concept is heat rises, but he knew it was not going to be that kind of heat.

The Metro Men began to fan themselves uncontrollably. The heat became so intense the first man started to do the robot. The second man screamed "*Hee, Hee!*" and began to moonwalk. The third man started to do the twist extremely slow as if he was the fat but famous chubby checker. The fourth man broke down and began to do the stripper booty clap dance. The distinct problem with his dance was he had no booty, no ass, no junk in the trunk, or a rump shaker. Alex had to turn his head because the dance was so disgusting his eyes began to fill with tears.

The man in the purple leg warmers seemed calm, cool and collected. He was not fanning or dancing but standing stationary with his back to the elevator door. His eyes began to bulge, and his lips began to pucker. He started to snap his fingers in a circular motion. Alex could see he gave up trying to hold his emotions inside. The man in the purple leg warmers began strutting like he was on the model's runway. He stopped strutting just before he bumped into Alex, who was crouched down in the back of the elevator. He paused, turned around, and started the process over sashaying violently back to the doors of the elevator.

The five Metro Men's activities in the elevator came to a stop because the next flavor shift was beginning. The heat had risen beyond any temperature he had ever experienced. He knew he may not survive the heat from the Habanero chili pepper flavor shift mixed with the three-week-old bowl of chili. Alex remembered that Stella left him with a burning desire. He could not do anything but stuff his face with the first thing he had in the fridge which was the old chili. He was sure they all would be "*Dead on Arrival*" when the elevator came to a stop on the l 0th floor.

Alex regretted eating his final meal until he heard Stella calling his name through the elevator shaft. He realized the elevator was coming to the 10th floor. Stella was going to be outside the elevator doors when it stopped. The men were motionless; their bodies were positioned as if they were toys that ran out of batteries. Their outfits were drenched with sweat, and their emotions seemed to be drained. The heat was subsiding, and there was a sense of euphoria in the elevator. The next flavor shift was beginning.

The Metro Men began to shake violently as if they were bitten by a venomous snake. Alex was still crouched in the fetal position at the back of the elevator. He tried to stop himself from shaking, but the heat from the Habanero chili pepper seemed to engulf his soul. The elevator came to a stop on the 10 the floor. The elevator doors opened, and Stella was standing with her arms opened wide. Alex used all of his remaining strength to clear a path through the five metro men and lunged toward Stella.

Stella sidestepped him like a football linebacker wearing 3-inch heels. She reached in the door, pushed the basement floor button and ensured the doors closed on the sweat-drenched, violently shaking Metro Men. Stella and Alex could hear the men screaming in horror at the Habanero chili pepper mixed with three-week-old chili smell. The screams became more and more intense as the elevator descended to the basement floor. The screams where disturbing because the Metro Men were screaming like little girls.

Stella gazed into Alex's eyes for a few moments to ensure he was alright. Suddenly, Stella turned Alex toward the office door and said, "*Get in there and get some work done you slacker.*" Alex followed her instructions without asking a question. During the workday, Alex left a sticky note on her desk asking her to walk him to his car. The end of the day came, and Stella was standing outside the office door ready to leave. When they entered the stairwell, Alex asked her the question. "*Is this why you fed me the hot peppers?*" Stella smiled and said, "*Let me explain.*"

Stella heard about the plot by The Metro Men Squad to steal what they called "*The Fragrant Fluffing Secret*" from her friend Amanda. She arrived at the lobby hoping to save Alex. The Metro Men just pushed her on an open elevator when they confirmed Alex was close to entering the lobby. Alex thanked Stella, and they embraced. He knew there was something about Stella that makes his heart flutter. He had never felt like this except when he would think about his mother.

Chapter 2

Getting Stella's Groove Back Wasn't That Easy

Stella and Alex became a hot item outside the office. Stella ensured that their work relationship did not change. She still was an outspoken proponent of Alex's old ways. She ensured that no one in the office would forget the previous Alex. Alex did not mind her continuing her antagonistic campaign against him because it gave him a chance to continue to play offense and launch verbal assaults against her overbearing persona.

Alex always wanted a sweet girl whom he could perform romantic escapades like his father used to carry through for his mother. Alex could tell Stella's feelings were getting stronger for him each day. Alex loved performing charming acts like his Father outside of work but still keep their work relationship in the same.

Alex began to imagine the creative things his dad did for his mother. They would watch his mom walking by the front window with some of her work colleagues at her office. Once they passed into another department. Alex and his father would make a beeline for the front door. His dad would walk up to the receptionist, place flowers and candy on the counter and say to the receptionist. "*I know my sweetie is in a very important meeting. Please ensure she gets these items and let her know her big strong men were here to deliver flowers and candy to her in her Daytime Jail, I mean work establishment*" Alex could still see the enormous smile the receptionist gave him as his dad turned and hurried out of the door and into his car.

Once they drove off, Alex and his father would celebrate by pulling off their collared shirts and swinging them like helicopters over our heads in the car. It took Alex years to figure out why mom would come home and literally smother us with love for at least a week. Mom loved my dad with such intensity I knew they would be together forever.

Stella cherished every moment with Alex. She had not been in a relationship with a man as thoughtful and caring as Alex. When she thought about Alex, she would begin to giggle like a schoolgirl. It was like she was having a teenage love affair. Stella would keep a memento from every excursion and write something in her diary each time Alex did something caring and thoughtful.

The next few weeks Alex provided her with encounters that only happens in romance novels and on the big screen. Stella would share her enchanting retreats with her closest friend Amanda. Amanda had been her best friend since grade school. Amanda was intrigued by their romantic dates but has a flaky personality. She is cute, so men initially would become attracted to her. Over a span of a couple of weeks, her real character would slowly surface.

Amanda has always been a moody, jealous, drama queen capable of throwing raging tantrums raster than a speeding bullet. The first couple of weeks are defined as the honeymoon stage. Once Amanda would show her true self it would be over. The men would quickly dump her using lame excuses. One of the best lame excuses came from this guy who told her "*My mom told me to leave you alone because you are not a keeper, you're the Grim Reaper!*" The majority of the men would drop off the radar not giving her any explanation. Amanda was completely oblivious to why men would not want to be with her because she considered herself a great catch.

The stories Stella would share with Amanda about flowers and walks on the beach were exciting to Amanda. She would hang on Stella's every word. Amanda would continuously tell Stella "*This guy is the one and only one for you.*" She would tease Stella by singing "*Dumb, Dumb, Dee, Dumb*" then Stella would start snickering like a young school girl. The only time Stella did not have great things to say about Alex was when she would tell the story about how she saves him from the Metro Men in the elevator.

Stella really wanted to know the exact details of his ordeal in the elevator. The problem was every time she would begin to question Alex about the Metro Men his facial expression would change. Alex would become perplexed and not be able to speak for at least a couple of hours. She noticed that his whole personality would change from sweet, charming and witty to somber and depressed. She got the impression, that what happened to him was so terrible that the experience emotionally crippled him

Amanda began to systematically ask Alex what happened in the elevator with the Metro Men. Alex would simply stop what he was doing, look her in the eyes and say, *"Go have a tantrum or something."* Amanda would immediately feel her temperature rise. Alex would then say, *"Can I help you with your wadded up panties?"* Amanda would not be able to control her anger and scream *"Stop pushing my buttons!"* Alex would say, *"Okay, I will get Stella to help you with pushing buttons and straightening out those wadded up panties."* Amanda would not be able to control her anger. She would end up throwing a mini tantrum or using her anger management techniques to avoid a major meltdown.

Stella would bring up the subject of Alex, the elevator, and the Metro Men to Amanda. Amanda would let her know Alex was perfect in every way, but there was something different about him. She always pointed out the changes Alex had been making to himself over the time they became an official couple. She pointed out how he started to keep his nails clean and manicured, regularly get haircuts, dress in a collared shirt, and wear Dockers instead of his customary blue jeans.

Stella asked herself *"Did something really happen to Alex in that elevator before she saved him?"* Stella turned to Amanda with tears in her eyes. Amanda immediately sensed her pain and began to let her know it was going to be alright. Amanda reminded Stella that she had a date with Alex in an hour. It was time for her to get ready for her Prince. They went to her room to pick out the perfect outfit for the romantic date she was about to have. Amanda began to call Stella *"Sleeping Booty"* the Princes waiting for the man from the sweet smelling Fluctuating Kingdom. They picked the perfect outfit with the perfect accessories and retired to the living room.

Stella and Amanda sat on the couch waiting for Alex to arrive. They stared at the clock impatiently. Alex was supposed to arrive at 5 pm. The clock read 5:03 and no Alex. Stella's heart sank, but Amanda was there to console her best friend. Amanda reminded Stella she will continue to be with her through thick and thin. The doorbell rang. The clock showed 5:10. Alex arrived ten minutes late. This was another change that Stella noticed because Alex was always obsessed with being on time in the past.

Amanda sprang to her feet, positioned herself at the door, and quickly swung the door open. Alex was standing upright wearing an olive-colored button down dress shirt with a simple floral pattern stitched in black with silver thread. Stella noticed he was also wearing a pair of black slacks with vertical olive-colored pinstripes. Stella loved how Alex's little belly gently pushed out just far enough passed the front of his pants to be noticeable. It reminded her of her father.

Her thoughts wandered to her father as she remembered some of the great times they shared. She would always sneak up on her father and grab his belly from behind. She would grab his midsection with her hands and hint that she needed a spare tire for her car. She could always feel his happiness when he embraced her. His warm personality and open heart ever made her feel safe and secure. Stella looked at Alex with the same admiration as her father. He was just like him in many ways. Stella placed her focus back on Alex.

Stella spent a long time gazing at him. She realized he was standing in the doorway holding a small white box in his left hand. The couple's eyes locked as Alex made his way to Stella. He stopped in front of her as she was sitting on the couch. He kneeled down on one knee and grabbed her hand.

Alex gently placed the small white box in her hand and covered it with his hand. Stella's eyes became affixed to their hands with the box hidden between their hands. Alex took a deep breath and put his right hand under Stella's chin and raised her face so he could gaze into her eyes.

Amanda seeing what was happening instinctively reacted to the romantic movie like situation. She walked over and snatched the box out of their hands. She grabbed Alex by the shirt and stood him up from his kneeling position. Amanda pushed Alex back outside the door of Stella's apartment. She took the box, pushed it into the middle of his chest and pushed him out into the hallway. Amanda looked into his eyes hoping to find some connection between them, but Alex's eyes turned to Stella. Amanda screamed loudly and slammed the door in his face with every ounce of strength she could muster.

Amanda turned to look at Stella. Stella was calmly staring at her hands as if the box was still resting in them. Amanda walked over and pulled her hands open calmly saying, "*It is too soon for that kind of behavior from him. There is something very wrong with this picture. He has got your number girlfriend.*" Stella's eyes opened widely as she looked at Amanda and broke down in tears.

The rest of the night the two women sat on the couch analyzing every detail of Stella and Alex's relationship. The ladies sat and discussed the relationship at great length. In the end, they both agreed that they had to get to the bottom of the elevator incident or the relationship would have to end. Stella thought to herself she is right. I am glad I have a close friend like Amanda. She has been there for me since grade school.

That night did not go as planned. The ladies could not shake the somber feelings; they were having. This lousy karma was producing an adverse effect upon the ladies, but Amanda suggested a solution. A girl's night out to relax and have some fun. She knew of a great little bar tucked away where drinks were cheap, and people were fun to be around.

Stella agreed to go. Stella gave Amanda a big hug and thanked her for being such a great friend.

The girls began to chant *"Let the primping begin!"* They started lady's night out by pouring each other a glass of wine. They turned on the music and danced the forbidden dance. They were dirty dancing on the couch and the coffee table but stayed away from the love seat. Amanda christened the toaster to ensure Stella would not outdo her. They tried on outfits, sang into their hair brushes, ordered pizza, and ate ice cream straight from the carton. It was lady's night out. The girls were having the time of their lives.

The next few hours the girls renewed their sense of womanhood. They were standing in the middle of the living room dressed to impress. Each of them took turns modeling the outfits which transformed them from girls to goddesses. Stella reached over and began to stroke Amanda's hair gently. She pulled her close and whispered softly in her ear. *"Call the cab you slut, I am sexier than you, and I am about to prove it."* Amanda reached into her back pocket and grabbed her cell phone. She held it up to her mouth and said, *"I got them on speed dial, you hussy. Keep stroking my hair because I am going to be stroking something longer and harder later."* Stella said, *"Yea, A tall glass filled with a Mojito!"*

The ladies walked out of the apartment building and entered the cab. They noticed that the driver was smiling because he knew he was in the presences of two goddesses. The cab driver drove off looking in his rear-view mirror observing the women. The cab driver tried to make conversation with the ladies. The ladies just looked at him and giggled like school girls. The driver eventually got the hint, and the ladies began to enjoy the beautiful summer night. The soft breeze was blowing toward the west, and the temperature was about 85 degrees Fahrenheit.

The cab driver saw the outline of a person out of the corner of his eye. He slammed on the breaks, and the cab stopped inches in front of the person. It was Mr. J the local transient standing in front of the cab waving his hands frantically. The cab driver put his head out the window yelled at him to get out the way, or he would turn him into a speed bump. Mr. J insisted that he was in need of a ride. He would not move because it was an emergency. He reached into his pocket and held up a wad of tattered dollar bills.

The ladies looked at each other and together told the cab driver to let him in. The cab driver looked over his shoulder and asked the ladies *"Are you sure?"* with a concerned look on his face. The ladies nodded their heads up and down to approve his entry into the cab. The cab driver motioned Mr. J to enter the passenger's side. Mr. J bounced up in the air, and seemingly glided over the front of the hood of the cab. He elegantly moved to the passenger-side door. He raised his leg and stuck it in the window and gently slid into the passenger's seat. Stella thought to herself He is quite graceful for a transient. Mr. J snapped his seat belt into position, placed his hands on the dash, and started to sing *"Keep on Moving do stop no"* in a low voice.

The cab driver rolled down all the windows in the cab and put the pedal to the metal. The tires spun out, and they were moving at a high rate of speed. The girls realized that the cab was filled with a foul odor. Transients do not have the greatest hygiene practices. The girls hugged each other close and covered their noses. The rush of air entering the cab with the windows rolled down was the only thing stopping them from jumping out of the moving vehicle because the smell was intense.

The cab driver turned into a race-car driver as he navigated through the city streets. Mr. J did not seem to mind. He was singing and dancing as the cab whipped left and right. The speed did not seem to bother him because he was grooving with the cab moving at Mach 90. When the cab made a sharp turn, Mr. J simply compensated with a smooth body movement and continued to groove to the song he was singing.

The cab driver slammed on the breaks as the cab came to an abrupt stop in the middle of the road. Mr. J. looked at the driver, smiled and said, *"That will be $13.50. Here is 16 dollars, keep the change My Brother from another Mother."* He looked over his shoulder to the back seat and said, *"Thanks for the ride Ladies!"* Mr. J slid out the window of the cab the same way he slipped into the cab and darted into a nearby alley. The cab driver stepped on the gas again jerking the ladies' heads back. He drove frantically for another two blocks and brought the cab to another sudden stop. The cab was in front of the bar. The cab driver rushed them out of the cab and let them know that Mr. J paid their cab fare.

The ladies entered the bar and just like Amanda stated there was a great mix of people. The DJ was playing music from the top 100 list. The ladies made their way to two empty seats at the bar. While sitting at the bar, they had two shots of tequila and a tall Mojito. The ladies began conversing with two charming, good-looking guys at a nearby table. Amanda was immediately attracted to the bad boy who was cracking jokes and making them laugh uncontrollably. Stella was having a witty conversation with the Knight in Shining Armor, who was intelligent and culturally refined. Over the next couple of hours, the two men took turns purchasing drinks, dancing with the ladies, and engaging in great conversation.

The night was young, and the goddesses were having the best ladies' night out ever. The Knight in Shining Armor seemed familiar to Stella. Stella felt she had met him before but could not place him after a couple of hours and too many drinks to count. The guys suggested they take a walk to get away from the loud music, smoke, and drunk people inside the bar. The ladies agreed to just a walk around the block.

The four of them left the bar and started down the sidewalk. Amanda was getting frisky with her bad boy. One city block of walking made them stop to make out while leaning on one of the parking meters. Stella and her man continued to stroll slowly as not to leave the playful new couple. The Knight suggested those two needed to get a room and Stella agreed. Stella felt as ease walking with her knight in shining armor.

He reached down and grabbed her hand as they walked. Stella did not disagree and felt that was a nice gesture. After another block, he gently placed his hand around her waist. He was so smooth that Stella could not stop herself from laying her head on his shoulder as they walked. Suddenly, with one quick motion, he guided her into an alley. A flash of memory came to her, and she remembered the Knight in Shining Armor was one of the men who shoved her in a nearby elevator during Alex's ordeal. She struggled to get away, but he was too strong. He brought her to an abrupt stop deep inside the alley.

Out of the darkness in the alley, the Metro Men appeared. They were not wearing bright colors anymore. The colors were replaced with earth tones. The guy with purple leg warmers was wearing faded purple skinny jeans. He spoke in a low raspy tone that sounded evil. He said, *"Stella did you really think you could cross my people. We will make you an example as we get our revenge."* Stella opened her mouth to scream for help, but nothing came out but a soft growl. The man in the faded purple skinny jeans snapped his fingers and said, *"Men prepare the wench for the shoot of her life."*

Simultaneously, the men snapped their fingers together in sync. One of the men reached over and grasped the top button of her blouse. He gently tugged as three buttons popped open just exposing the cleavage portion of her bra and the meaty part of her breasts. The other two positioned her body in a provocative pose. The Knight placed his face as if he was kissing her cleavage. Then it happened! A flash of light pulsated through the alley. They moved her to a standing position. One man reached over and gently tugged on the button of her tight-fitting jeans. Stella heard the button pop open, and her zipper began to the fall lower and lower. Two men grabbed her jeans on each side, and she felt a gentle tug downward. The men bent her over just enough to expose the lace of her skimpy panties.

The Knight took the lace from the panties grasped it with

his teeth and smiled. A flash of light pulsated through the alley again. Every time, the leader would say, *"Bang"* They would move her in a different provocative position. The positions were changing with such grace that she was amazed at how gentle the men treated her. She tried to scream but simply let out another soft growl. Stella was helpless to stop the photo shoot. In her mind, she prayed for a miracle. The men suddenly released their grasp on her. She fell to the ground barely catching herself with her arms. The Metro Men were running out of the alley. Why? She could see someone running in the dark. The Metro Men were in hot pursuit of the dark figure. She could hear the figure screaming, in the distance *"Thanks for the ride lady!"*

She quickly gathered herself and made her way back to the bar. Amanda was sitting at the table crying with a drink in her hand. Stella grasped her by the hand and led her out of the bar as fast as her feet would take her. Amanda told Stella we cannot leave; my bad boy is coming back for me. Stella hailed a cab and jumped in quickly. The cab ride home was quiet. The ladies sat at opposite ends of the backseat of the cab. There was no conversation. The night was over, and the ladies' night out came to an abrupt end.

Chapter 3

A Leader Questions His Desire

Looking in the mirror at the face he had seen for twenty-something years. The pronounced cheekbones, strong looking chin, and jet-black hair made him feel superior to all men. He is a perfect gentleman, with an IQ of 126, and a superb sense of style. He leaned forward to get as close to the mirror as possible. *"Isn't your street name P-luscious!"* I am the only man in the world with enough fashion sense to pull off the purple leg warmers with any outfit. My given name is Ignacio, *"No last name required."*

Ignacio found himself questioning his leadership for the first time. During the last two years every goal he set for himself and the Metro Man ended in a success. The recent missed opportunities really made his leadership look like he was not the best of the best. He could blame the first missed opportunity on the members who discussed valuable information with outsiders, not in *"The circle of trust."*

He glared in the mirror and said, *"A transient foiled the plan."* The plan was perfect. Get the girl. Snap some black male photos. Use her to get the secret from Alex. Get revenge for her part in the elevator torcher chamber. The ride down to the basement was so horrible with the heat, the smell, and the mental anguish. All articles of clothing had to be burned, and Ignacio had to pay for spa treatments for all Metro Men.

Ignacio held his fist in the air because he did not anticipate the transient jumping out the shadows of the alley, snatching the camera out of his hands, and running through the streets. The Metro Men chased him for over 30 minutes. The transient was toying with them as they chased him but could not catch him. He was screaming thanks for the ride lady's over and over. The transient stopped under a street light and did the Macarena dance for a few brief moments with the camera. The transient raised the camera over his head and spiked the camera like a football. The metro men froze as they watched the camera shatter into pieces. The transient let out a scream and fell to his knees as if he made a mistake. He ran into the darkness laughing loudly like a madman.

The Metro Men ran for the camera hoping they could salvage the memory card in the camera. Maybe the memory card could have been recovered. They picked up every piece of the camera off the ground. The camera was broken beyond repair. The memory card was never located. The transient got the first and the last laugh by foiling the plan. Ignacio watched as his handpicked Metro Men lost their desire. The silence between them was unbearable because Metro Men always have something to say. They consistently get the last word, whether you like it or not.

Metro Men are not fighters or lovers. It's all about the id, the ego, and the superego. The life of a Metro Man is based upon their ability to gain accolades for their contribution to the beautiful people in the world. They are not so tough that they will not haul off and punch you in the face like a regular man. If it is another handsome man they just reach over slap you and throw little girly punches like the other men.

The Metro Man rule of thumb is as follows; no physical contact, no ripping beautiful clothing, and no four-letter words. Insults have to be intelligently and eloquently vetted. The way they settled their disputes is a dance-off or a model pose down. The Metro Men really knew how to strut their stuff Ignacio *"P- luscious"* last name not required is the self-proclaimed King of the Metro World. He felt he was only second to the King of Pop and he is in heaven.

Mr. P-Luscious needed a plan that would get his revenge on Stella, the transient, and to get the fluffing secret from Alex. This plan would have to be perfect because his reputation as the leader of the Metro Men was on the line. He had never been a follower and shuttered at the thought of being second in command of the Metro Men he started. The worst-case scenario to be banished into seclusion and never seen or heard from again. The thought of retiring his signature purple leg warmers caused him to become engulfed in making the perfect plan.

Mr. P-luscious knew three things had to take place for his plan to get back on track. The first order of business was to hit Stella in her weak spot hard and heavy. He knew after last night; she would want to keep that particular lady's night out a secret from Alex. He needed to get Alex to a weakened state because he had heard the story about the box, the knee, and then the slammed door that occurred between Amanda, Stella, and Alex. That situation would provide Mr. P-luscious a considerable leverage point in his negotiation for the fluffing secret. Third, the wild card of the situation was the transient. Who? What? When? Where? and How? He thought to himself a transient is the lowest of low in society. A simple gesture of a dollar figure, drugs, alcohol a warm place to sleep and/or an anonymous call to the police would get him the advantage he needed.

Mr. P-luscious was planning the most important mission of his life. He realized that if the plan failed, he would lose Angelina, his girlfriend. Angelina is considered the Greek goddess of love mixed with the beautiful *"Aphrodite."* He did not even have to wine and dine her because it was understood the most beautiful people in society would naturally be together. He considered it a natural selection.

P-luscious recalled the first time a rival female tried to tempt him with her goodies. He politely requested she leave him alone because Angelina was the only woman for him. The woman kept pushing for his attention and was literally pressing all of her goodies against any body part she could touch and/or rub on Mr. P-luscious body.

Angelina heard about the woman and confronted her outside the dance studio on Main Street. During the altercation, the woman quickly realized she was outmatched. She looked around at the crowd that was gathering as if someone was going to help her. The woman panicked and attempted to flee the situation may be hoping to regroup to strike another day. Angelina paused for a few seconds as she adjusted her outfit. Angelina was wearing a sheer black blouse accentuated with a lavender lace bra, black leather mini skirt, black fishnet stockings and black 6-inch stilettos. The outfit was accented with all 24-karat gold accessories.

Angelina pursued her with such grace and style the crowd was mesmerized. She ran the rival woman down gracefully, kicked her butt utilizing a form of martial arts called Kandoshin. She did not even perspire or breathe heavy. There was not one hair out of place, and her outfit was still looking stunning. Angelina sashayed back basking in the attention she was receiving from the crowd that had accumulated.

P-luscious took off half a workday to get the plan in place. He first called Angelina and invited her on a date. He assured Angelina, there would be fine dining, dancing and passionate love to end the night. This may be the last time he would be able to bask in the presences of a goddess and wanted to ensure he had the chance to fulfill all his fantasies before the plan was set in motion. The second call was to the Bad Boy. P-luscious knew bad boy needed to finish what he started with Amanda.

The Bad Boy loves the ladies. He knows he is God's gift to women and is trying to make love to every woman he can. He is the master of using his crazy, fun loving personality to get to the ladies' goodies. There is no size, color, weight, character, marital status or body type he preferred. They just had to be classified as a woman, and he would do all he could to get busy with them. P-Luscious set up a meeting.

The two men discussed his vital role in the plan. The bad boy was his street name, but in the Metro Man Circle of Trust, his name was *"Horn Dog."* This name was only used in occasions when the women he romanced had unique characteristics. The unique features did include blind, crippled and crazy but everyone knew the bad boy loves the ladies.

The bad boy agreed to his role in the plan and was ready

to fall on the sword for his great leader. The bad boy knew Amanda would fit in the crazy woman category so he would not get the benefits that come with dating the blind or crippled like handicapped parking. P-luscious hung up the phone and began to get ready for what could be his last night with the goddess of love. The wheels of the plan were set in motion, and he knew he would have to spend a significant amount of money to make his goddess do the things he had on his fantasy list.

Chapter 4

Can She Push The Knife Deep Into Stella's Back?

Amanda's eyes opened. She was waiting for the imminent hangover that follows nights like last night. She went over the weekend party checklist in her head. A migraine headache nowhere to be found. Dragon Breath was still in the Dark Kingdom, and not in her mouth. Last night's clothes were still on her body but were pretty wrinkled. Makeup still on her face but is probably smeared from the bouts of crying. Memories of last night were intact, and depression was setting in already. She was alone in the bed again. A tear began to form in the corner of her eye.

Amanda jumped out of bed before starting another bout of heavy crying. She started getting herself cleaned up both physically and emotionally because last night was a rough night. As she made her way to the bathroom, her mind wandered to the Bad Boy. She was missing being held in his loving arms. She could feel a passion building between them that could last forever at least in her world. She remembered a crowd of people stopped to watch them make out, which fueled their passion.

Amanda knew he was Mr. Right because even onlookers could see their love for each other. The Bad Boy asked that they slow down because he had to take care of some personal business. He asked her to meet him back at the bar, so he could go to the bathroom and get a pack of cigarettes. Amanda agreed and went back to the bar to wait for his return. She did not know how many drinks she had while waiting for him, but she knew he was coming back for her.

Amanda said to herself in the mirror *"That dumb wench*

Stella made me leave the bar in a rush." No explanation! She just grabbed me and forced me to leave the bar. Amanda thought to herself. She probably let her Knight in Shining Armor bang her in the alley. He apparently pulled her hair and smacked her ass over and over until she screamed in ecstasy. Stella probably felt guilty because she has the best of both worlds. She has one man for romance and one man for raw, passionate escapades. I have no man and will have to listen to twice as many of the stories Stella will be telling.

The phone began to ring. Amanda ran across the room and snatched her cell phone off the counter. She glanced at the caller ID. It was Stella. She could feel her anger building, but she calmed herself and said, *"Hello Stella, How is it hanging?"* in a steady but monotone voice. Stella apologized for her actions last night. Amanda requested an update on what happened between her and the Knight in Shining Armor. Stella said they would talk soon, but she had to discuss it with her mother before she was ready to let her in on what happened. Amanda pressed the end call button on her cell phone, then slammed the phone down on the counter in anger. Amanda thought that was a bunch of crap. Stella has not talked to her mother in years. She is a daddy's girl. Amanda folded her arms and began to try to stop herself from throwing a tantrum.

The room was silent as Amanda desperately tried to stop her anger from the building. She heard a strange sound. It was a clicking sound. It was someone throwing small rocks at her window. She heard it again. She stomped over to the window and whipped it open. She stuck her head out the window and screamed: *"Stop throwing rocks at my window."* When she looked to see who it was, she realized the Bad Boy had found her. It was him standing in the street looking up at her with his arms spread as if he wanted to give her a great big hug. Bad Boy screamed *"AMANDA CAN YOU COME OUT AND PLAY!"* Amanda screamed: *"YES!"* and asked for ten minutes, so she could get ready. She closed the windows and ran into the shower, dove into some jeans, slid into a blouse, no bra needed, and quickly threw on some eyeliner and ruby-red lipstick which made her beautiful for her new man.

She ran down to her man who was waiting for her in the street. The Bad Boy took her to this charming little restaurant that served the best chili in town. Amanda was happy because the sparks of passion were still there from the previous night. They kissed, snuggled, played footsie under the table. The chili was good too but having a man who truly loved her was priceless. Amanda was having a wonderful time. It had been a long time since she was in love and she did not want to lose that loving feeling. The new couple agreed to go back to her place for a nightcap and seal the deal

The new couple was leaving the restaurant, and the Bad Boy received a phone call. He asked Amanda to stand at the door until he finished with his call. Amanda was standing in front of the door. She observed Alex walking down the street through the restaurant window. He crossed the road, and she realized he was heading straight for the restaurant. She panicked and realized that if she moved away from the main doors, she might miss her new man's return.

She watched Alex run up the front steps. The main door opened, and their eyes met. It seemed like there was about two minutes of awkward silence between them, but it was only a few moments. Amanda realized in those few moments that she knew everything about Alex through that lying two-faced slut Stella. She knew everything about Alex's romantic escapades, his personality, and his family.

Chapter 5

Alex Gets Back In The Saddle For The Ride Of His Life

Alex walks into the main door of his favorite restaurant. He immediately finds himself locked into an intense gaze with his girlfriend's best friend. He blinked, and the door was suddenly closed. Alex was just standing there with the box he had for Stella in his hand. Alex had a roll of money in his pocket for a romantic dinner. He made reservations for a horse and carriage ride through the city. The trip was going to end in front of the city's water attraction which is a wishing well. This was the perfect end to a perfectly planned adventure. Alex realized he was clutching the box over his heart with such force that it was beginning to collapse under the pressure. Amanda's face slowly faded back into his eyesight.

Alex and Amanda were speechless for a few seconds. Amanda reached up softly tugged on his ear and said, "How's my little trooper." Alex could not control his smile. Alex reached over and ran his fingers through her hair and smiled without even thinking. He then moved past her and sat in his regular seat where he always grabbed a bowl of chili.

Sitting at his regular table, he allowed himself to enjoy Amanda's hot little body. Whatever was between her ears was counterproductive to the beautiful assets she possessed physically. Her personality was like the most terrifying roller coaster with an extremely scary to ride. Alex figured if and when he had an opportunity to enjoy the forbidden fruits, he would decline the offer. He learned one of the greatest lessons from his father which was to focus one woman at a time.

Alex was really being romantic with the thoughts floating

around in his head. Alex never let himself take advantage of the forbidden fruits while he was with Stella. He only wanted to focus on Stella while they were together. When they were apart, he would plan his next romantic escape. Alex was not sure they were still a couple, so his upcoming passionate escape was an excellent bowl of chili. He did not hear from Stella for almost 24 hours. He was slowly turning back to his old self. He may not get a lot of chicks, but he sure had a lot of laughs at their expense.

He watched Amanda leave with a tall guy who had a slender athletic build. He looked familiar, for some reason. Just for a moment, Alex was jealous of the guy until he remembered the tantrums, he watched her throw in the past. Amanda looked over her shoulder and waved goodbye. Alex returned the gesture wondering how long she was going to keep that guy. Maybe he could give the guy some advice. Let him know he had about two weeks to stick it to her forbidden fruits because they are going to be rotten on the 15th day.

The waitress placed the bowl of chili in front of Alex. The thought of Amanda faded away as the smell of the delectable culinary prize filled his mind. He was salivating at the mouth like a dog going through Pavlov's classical conditioning in the investigation of Psychic Secretion. The sight of the bowl of chili loaded with sour cream, three types of cheeses, chives, red and black beans made him sit-up at attention. Alex grabbed the spoon, closed his eyes and said a prayer. *"Dear God, Thank you for this meal. This is the day I reclaim my life. I will eat healthier, dress superior, and be an improved person. I realize this bowl of comfort food is stopping me from becoming the best person I can be. This may be my last bowl."* Alex opened his eyes, put the spoon on the table and walked out of the restaurant without even eating a spoon full.

Alex went to the grocery store and purchased healthy foods. He stocked his kitchen cabinets with the items to lead an improved life. He went to the gym where he worked out with his newly hired personal trainer. After his workout he went home took a power nap and decided to go to the local pub to relax and do some much needed socializing.

Alex entered the pub and sat at the bar. He ordered water with lemon because he was still a little dehydrated from his work out. A few minutes went by, and a cute blonde came and sat in the seat next to him. She was making small talk, and Alex really had her attention. He flirted with her and kept her laughing with his offbeat humor. Alex asked for her name and number. She introduced herself as Julie and used her cell phone to beam her phone number to his cell phone. He never had luck with women, but this was the new Alex.

Alex and Julie were immersed in great conversation when suddenly; he felt a hand on his back. He looked over his shoulder and noticed it was Amanda. She moved her hand up his back to his ear. She tugged his ear again and said, *"Hey buddy."* Alex could not control his smile because Amanda was comforting him just like his mother would do.

Amanda raised her hand and ordered a scotch on the rocks with a dash of lime. Surprisingly, she selected Alex's favorite drink on her first attempt. Amanda said, "Hi to Julie", but they did not exchange names. They shook hands in a dainty way all women shake hands just before a catfight. Amanda announced she was going to mingle for a while. She suggested Alex enjoy his drink and his company. Alex thought to himself *"What the hell is going on?"* That was not the Amanda he knew. She was suddenly nice and polite. She knew just how to make him feel comfortable with the tug of the ear.

Julie asked him if Amanda was an ex-girlfriend. Alex told her *"Hell No! I have never seen that person in my life even though they have been acquaintances for five years. She is just a friend who he had not really gotten along with before today."* Alex quickly regrouped and cracked a joke about hoping not to have to give up his virginity to her because she bought him a drink. Julie giggled, and the conversation began to move forward again. Alex realized he had a lot in common with Julie and was happy he had her phone number. Julie paused for a moment then asked him to hold her seat at the bar while she went to go to the Ladies room. She needed to powder her nose and make a phone call to check on one of her sick friends.

Alex took a sip of his free drink and placed the glass on the bar. He felt a soft hand begin stroking his back. Amanda was standing behind him. She moved to the seat next to him and smiled. Amanda said, *"I did not know you liked blondes. I hope her lack of brains is not getting in the way of your conversation."* Alex smiled and laughed. He was speechless because who was this person sitting next to him. It undoubtedly was not the Amanda he knew through his girlfriend, maybe ex-Stella.

Amanda started a conversation on healthy eating and working out. Alex found it comforting to talk to Amanda about his plans to become a better person mentally and physically. She was listening to him attentively and never once insulted him like she had in the past. Amanda reached over tugged on his ear and ordered him another drink. Amanda let him know she could feel her slut meter was going off in her head. She needed to continue to mingle with the crowd. Alex looked over her shoulder, and Julie was headed towards her seat. Amanda casually walked off into the group.

Julie sat down in her seat. Alex asked how her friend was doing. Julie explained her friend was going through a rough patch in life, but she would be in a better place shortly. Julie really turned up the heat when it came to the conversation they were having. She began to ask precise questions about his preferences. Alex was happy to answer because this was the first time a woman seemed genuinely interested in him as a person. Julie blatantly told Alex she really liked him and would like to see him another time. She hinted that he should call her tomorrow to ensure they connected for the second time.

Julie revealed that she was not needy or looking for a relationship but felt like they should hook up and have some fun. Alex agreed and gave her his phone number. She looked out the window and hurriedly got up and left out the front door of the pub. She did not even look back which Alex thought was odd. Alex thought it was for the best because he was checking out her cute pockets on the tight stretch pants she was wearing. Alex said to himself, she is probably a stocker or drama queen and laughed to himself.

Alex turns to sip his free drink and watched Amanda sashay over to his side. She once again made him feel comfortable before Alex realized Amanda was ordering him another drink. This time she placed her hand on his inner thigh as she ordered him another drink. Alex smiled to himself as he thought about Amanda's forbidden fruit expiring on the 15th day. He realized she was saving him money, and that meant he would have enough money to purchase the three-ply heavy bag, thermal condoms, and a body bag. Amanda reached over and tugged at his ear and whispered: "*I see you are having a good time.*" She put her hand back on his thigh, but suddenly she gripped it. Alex jumped and smiled uncontrollably because Amanda was really making it hard for him to resist her advances.

The pub became quiet, and a familiar voice was calling Amanda's name. Alex and Amanda could hear Stella calling Amanda from across the pub. Amanda jumped out of her seat, and the women closed the gap between them in a hurry. They were face to face in the middle of the pub. They started saying words only sailors say while they are out to sea on a ship. Alex knew there was going to be a catfight. Alex did not move because he was scared the women would stop focusing on each other and turn on him. The argument escalated as Amanda said, "*Check Mate Stella.*" I can see your other man is standing behind you. There was a tall, good-looking man, with long blonde hair looking at Stella with a smile. Stella seemed to freeze like a statue. The blonde guy walked over and gave her a hug and a kiss on the lips.

Alex realized his heart was melting, and everything was moving in slow motion. Alex turned his head to stop looking at this man hugging the woman he wined and dined for weeks. He peered out the front window of the pub hoping he could just teleport out to the street. He noticed Mr. J. getting ready to jump out on the road in front of a moving cab. He was holding his hands in the air gripping a couple of tattered greenbacks.

Alex heard Stella scream and turned just as she grabbed a handful of Amanda's hair and jerked it with all of her strength. She reached back and started to scratch the good-looking guys face with her nails. The handsome guy lets out a feminine scream, and Alex recognized the guy from his ordeal in the elevator. Alex jumped out of the bar stool and made a beeline for the front door. He could clearly see Mr. J gesturing at him to hurry through the window of the pub. Alex glanced back, and all three people were engaged in an all-out war.

Alex ran out the pub door, and there was Mr. J. with the cab door open motioning him to get into the back seat. Alex jumped in, and Mr. J slammed the door behind him. Mr. J reached into the cab window grabbed Alex by the collar of his shirt and said, "*Aren't you going to thank me for the ride lady?*" The cab driver drove off before Alex could say anything. Alex watched as Mr. J walked over to the window of the pub throwing punches like he was shadow boxing the air.

Chapter 6

Mr. J Gets A Chance To Do The Forbidden Dance!

Mr. J could hear the sound of the car driving by the alley and the smell of Clair's bakery. He was waking up slowly. He reflected upon all the events that occurred after he politely helped Alex hail a cab. Mr. J realized he was a little groggy from the harsh night. He had the strange feeling that people were staring at him. He heard a soft voice say, *"He is sleeping like a newborn baby."* He heard a manly voice say, *"It must be the aroma of the fresh bread that is filling the air."* He heard a feminine voice say, *"No, it's the sound of trucks being filled with goodies and being driven off leaving exhaust in the alley for him to breathe."*

Mr. J found himself being awakened by the same two shop owners in the same alleyway every morning. Clair owned the bakery. Bruce owned the delivery service. Mr. J. never knows how he gets back to this alleyway, but he has been waking up in the alley every day since he can remember. He remembers nothing about his life before being awakened by Bruce, who almost ran him over with his first delivery truck.

It was a red 98 Dodge Ram fully loaded. Bruce tried to run Mr. J away from the alley but decided to let him stay after he realized Mr. J was useful. Bruce's truck would not start two weeks after he had been barreling out of the alley at top speeds. Bruce just kept on turning the engine over. Mr. J got so irritated that he jumped out of his makeshift bed, walked over to the driver side of the door, and pushed Bruce over to the passenger seat. He turned the radio channel to his favorite 80's pop music station then he stepped out of the truck, popped the hood, and performed all the simple mechanical checks. Surprisingly, one of the wires to the alternator cap was loose, so he pulled some tools out of the back of Bruce's truck and tinkered with it. He jumped back in the driver's seat and turned the ignition key. The truck started, and the engine purred like a cat. Mr. J. grabbed Bruce by his collar and pulled him back into the driver's seat. Mr. J closed the door, looked Bruce dead in the eyes and thanked him for the ride. He walked to his home in the alley and went back to sleep.

Mr. J realized he was coming back to reality. He had the strange feeling that people were staring at him. He could hear whispers then complete silence came over the alley. Bruce screamed loudly *"It is bath time sleeping beauty and doused him with a bucket of water."* The voices he heard became deafening as the mob grabbed him. They stood him up and spread his arms and legs. Mr. J tried to struggle, but the people in the crowd held him as others scrubbed him with soap. He felt as if he was going to drown. Mr. J tried to scream, but he was so terrified that he could only let out a soft growl. Never wanting to give up, he continued to try and yell, but the soft growl kept coming out of his mouth over and over. The soft growling sound really amused the mob that was force bathing him.

The employees for Claire's bakery and Bruce's delivery service would come by once a week to help provide Mr. J. with a weekly opportunity to perform excellent cleaning hygiene. The men would subdue, wash, scrub, rip clothes off, and wrap him in a large beach towel. The women would comb hair, lotion body parts, cut nails, and clean any scrapes and/or scratches.

Bruce would shove him into the bathroom to allow him to perform his essential personal hygiene that only he could perform. Claire would leave a set of clean clothes in the bathroom sink. When he was ready to go back out on the streets, he would come out the bathroom and stand at attention. Claire would inspect him like a drill sergeant. Mr. J had never passed the mouth and teeth inspection on the first try. She sent him back to the bathroom three times until he brushed them to her liking. He gargled until his breath smelled like forest rain. Claire only allowed him to return to the alley when she felt he was clean.

Mr. J was happy to be back in his alley after passing Drill Sergeant Claire's inspection. He closed his eyes, clicked his heels together, and chanted *"There is no place like home."* Claire screamed out the back of her bakery for him to stop acting out, or she would make him go through it again. Mr. J was happy to be clean as he took the time to enjoy being home in the alley. He specifically relished the sounds from the neighborhood streets and the smell of Claire's baked goods. There have been countless times he was gussied up by the cleaning team. Bruce and Claire tried to help him become normal but gave up when they realized his intelligence level far exceeded both of theirs combined.

Mr. J started to remember what happened at the bar as he was walking to watch the fight in the pub. He saw Stella's Aura exploded to bright yellow with a green outline. Two bolts of energy flew in the pub through the main window and slammed into Stella's body. The flashes of energy knocked the color out of her Aura. Alex could see me clearly through the pub window, so I began to hail him to the cab.

Calm came over Stella as if the bolts of energy gave her some sort of tranquilizer. Something crazy was going to happen because her Aura was gone, and some kind of power had taken over her body. Suddenly, Stella executed the coolest ninja move on the blonde man and woman standing next to her. She pulled the woman's hair and scratched the blonde guy's face so hard and fast with such violence it looked like a Coed Mixed Martial Arts Cat fight.

Mr. J began to walk to the window; he witnessed the second coolest ninja move. Stella's hand began to glow blue as she started reversing the primary ninja move by jerking Amanda's hair causing a whiplash effect towards the blonde guy. Stella grabbed a handful of the blonde guy's hair for leverage and began to scratch Amanda's face. It was beautiful, graceful and precise for a girl with blue glowing hands. He named it the Ninja Reversed Deluxe move for the Bar Fly.

The blonde guy was visibly bleeding bright-red blood from his face as he attempted to bear hug Stella. Amanda tried to move backward to get away from Stella's shredding claws. Stella performed a special Mixed Martial Arts move again. She wrapped her legs around the girl's waist and started ripping plugs of hair out of the blonde man's head and clawing the girls face.

Mr. J observed a burst of blue color come out of Stella's body. The crowd covered his view of the Ménage et Butt Kicking. Mr. J could hear screaming and yelling. The doors of the pub slammed open, and two female bodies went flying into the clear space in front of the pub. The two women were flying through the air. They landed on the edge of the sidewalk close to the street. The bouncer looked out the pub door to measure the distance, he threw the women. The crowd that followed him out of the bar screamed: *"That is a new record!"*

The bouncer walked back in the bar. Close to where the blonde guy was standing. The bouncer looked at his bleeding face, shook his hand and walked back inside the pub. The bouncer raised his hands in the air, and the crowd cheered. The blonde guy took a step down on the stairs, and two smaller bouncers from the pub grabbed him and threw him off the remaining steps. The crowd cheered loudly and went back to the pub.

Mr. J witnesses Stella, the Ninja Barfly stood up and began to walk towards the street. He recalled seeing her with Alex, so he used his unique talent to hail her a cab with tattered dollars in hand. A cab stopped in front of him, the Ninja Barfly came to the door. Suddenly, she grabbed him and fell backward into the cab's back seat bringing Mr. J with her. Their legs were dangling out the cab when the cab driver began to drive off. Mr. J quickly made sure they were both in the cab and closed the door.

Mr. J. noticed her hands were not glowing anymore, but she had a death grip on his matted hair, and she had her legs wrapped firmly around his waist. Mr. J realized he was in the back seat of a cab on top of a woman with her legs wrapped around his waist. He decided to pull away, but it was like she was dead and rigor mortis had set into her body. Every time, he tried to pull away her grip became stronger.

Mr. J began to panic and could feel himself start to hyperventilate. Mr. J. opened his eyes as wide as possible. He could see her Aura color turn to pure white so decided to relax and go with the flow. He got his breathing under control and began to breathe in sync with the woman. Mr. J notice her body slowly lost its pure white color as her death grip slowly began to subside. Mr. J fully relaxed his whole body as he cleared his mind of all thoughts.

Stella's grip became lenient, but Mr. J's mind began to drift. He could see himself flying through the clouds in the sky. He landed in front of a beautiful house with a white picket fence, green grass, yellow flowers and one of those cool Golf Guy Statues on the lawn. He opened the front gate and walked to the front of the door which was painted a fire-engine red. He rang the doorbell, and the door became transparent. He could see a family with a boy and girl and a familiar looking woman sitting on the couch. The boy jumped up, ran and looked out the window. He yelled *"Daddy's home"* and reached over to open the door. The young boy and Mr. J's eyes locked in a gaze.

The cab came to an abrupt stop breaking his meditative state. Stella kicked the door open and pushed her way out of the cab. She still had a hand full of Mr. J's hair, so he had no choice but to exit the cab with her. Stella recognized her neighborhood and could see the door to her apartment. She released the death grip on his hair and began stumbling toward the front door of the building. Mr. J notices her Aura was glowing a soft blue color. He looks down and sees; he is flickering the same color, but his tone quickly subsides. Stella was still glowing as she made her way to the door of her building.

He thought to himself that crazy Ninja Barfly drained all my energy while I was in a meditative state. He made a mental note to himself. Never become Captain Save a Hoe. On no account lay on top of a helpless woman in the backseat of a cab. Under no circumstances allow your soft blue essence to be stolen by performing acts of heroism during times of violent outbursts in public.

Mr. J could feel his life force leaving his body. He was so tired and realized he was getting tunnel vision. The light at the end of the tunnel was closing rapidly. He needed to get back to his home. His legs began to move toward the light at the end of the tunnel. He started counting each step he took in his mind. One, two, three, four, five, six, seven. He hoped he could make it back to his humble dwelling in the alley.

The alley seemed so far as he was still counting twenty-one, twenty-two, and twenty-three. He could feel himself crawling on the ground struggling to get to his humble abode. He could hear familiar voices but could not identify the people as he still counted the numbers fifty-one, fifty-two, fifty-three.

Suddenly, he felt safe as he felt a soft kiss press against his cheek. He recognized the person's scent but could not place the name or picture as to how the person looked. Mr. J. heard one of the voices say, *"Can we keep him?"* He could hear sounds and smell the scents of the alley. That was the moment he knew he made it home again but was he really home?

Chapter 7

Will There Be A New Sheriff In Town?

Alex jumped out of the cab and ran up to his apartment. His mind was racing because he was thankful Mr. J saved him from the situation inside the pub. He had no way of contacting Mr. J to show his gratitude but would make it a point to thank him in person.

Alex opens the door to his apartment and looks around happily because he made it home in one piece. He decided the best course of action was to perform the three Ss. (Sh*t, Shower, and Shave) He decided tonight was going to be the movie, beer, and popcorn night. Alex had seen enough drama for the rest of the week. He was going to ensure there would be no drama because he was going to keep a low profile until the end of the week.

He decided his first mission in the morning was to thank Mr. J. with a crisp 20-dollar bill and a big ole hug. Alex knew he would have to throw his clothes away after hanging out with the transient philosopher. Transients do not have the best hygiene practices. It would be worth the torturous effort to show his undying gratitude for saving him from one of life's crazies past times "DRAMA!"

Alex slept in late the next morning, probably closer to brunch. Alex really needed lunch more than breakfast because he was craving a bowl of chili. The taste of the chili was so strong in his mouth it overpowered the three-headed dragon that normally was in his mouth. Alex really knew he was going to have his work cut out for himself not to give in to his urges. The taste of chili was so loud even toothpaste, mouthwash, and breath mints still tasted like a fresh bowl of chili. Alex continued on his mission to perform a perfect Three S night, but first, he had to stand and apply torque before his hygiene ritual. His expert skills allowed him to have a perfect shot into the Porcelain Gods' Throne. After twenty minutes he competed the perfect three S ritual and was ready to leave on his adventure.

Alex knew he had to get moving because he had no idea where Mr. J. lived. Making an educated guess from the conversations he had with Mr. J. He entered the neighborhood where he felt he could locate Mr. J. He stopped at a few local small businesses and asked questions like a private investigator asking for information. They all let him know that he needed to find Claire who owned the neighborhood bakery. Alex noticed that many of the store owners smile and mentioned Mr. J's bath, but he just dismissed it.

Alex located the bakery that Claire owned and operated. He walked in the front door to see a slightly plump attractive woman smiling at him. Alex said, *"Hi, you must be Ms. Claire."* Claire stated that she had been getting phone calls for the past hour about some guy who wanted to give Mr. J. a reward for doing a good deed. Claire let Alex know that he lived in the alley. Claire mentioned that Mr. J had the bare essentials he needed. She went on to explain how mentally, physically, intellectually, mechanically, and interpersonally advanced Mr. J's persona is compared to the rest of the population. She still could not figure out why he was the smartest knife outside of the drawer.

Alex thanked Claire for the information and began to leave the shop to head around the block to get to the alley. Claire stopped Alex from going out the front door by running from behind the counter and grabbing him by the hand. She then guided him through the bakery to the back door. She gave him a kiss on the cheek and shuffled him out the back door of the bakery.

Alex entered the alley as the police escorted Mr. J into a police car. Another policeman was speaking with the purple leg warmer guy from the elevator. The guy was wearing a pair of rusty off purple jeans, a shiny white button-down shirt and a Fedora tilted to the side of his head.

Alex immediately felt a rush of anxiety flowing from his stomach as he surveyed the situation. Alex noticed there was a woman in the alley with a boy watching the scene develop with a concerned look on her face. The purple leg warmer man was talking to the policeman. Alex could see he was lying because he kept rubbing his face and looking to the right every time the police officer asked him a question. He could not hear what they were talking about, but he knew it had to about his transient friend.

Mr. J was standing at the passenger's side door of the police car screaming *"Officer Badge number 23789 will be escorting me to the police station. The girly man who is giving a statement to Officer Badge number 13457 put me in a frame. I am innocent before proving to be guilty, but in the meantime, I get three Hot's with dollar days baby."* Mr. J slid into the passenger-side window of the police car. He snapped his seat belt and assumed his normal riding position.

Alex could feel his anxiety build because the events seemed to unsettle his nerves. His mind was racing as he continued to survey the situation. Claire came out of the back door of the bakery and screamed *"Unhand cuff my friend!"* Claire ran toward the police car screaming *"Let him go!"* The two policemen saw Claire running towards the police car stopped the questioning entered their vehicles and sped away.

Seeing all this drama unfolding Alex's anxiety was building to a level he never experienced throughout his life. His body just began to run behind Claire chasing her but just before he passed the purple leg warmer man his body did something he had never done before. It was like he was having an out of body experience. Alex's mind immediately focused on purple leg warmer man's ear. Alex could see himself throw a left cross punch that connected with the girly man's ear.

This punch was thrown with the entire force of his body at a full forward running stride. He watched as his fist connected dead center on the Metro Man's ear. The man's head snapped sideways, and the Fedora flew off his head. It seemed like the hat flew fifty feet before it hit the ground. Alex looked back at the man hit the ground in slow motion. Alex realized he threw his first devastating punch. Alex looked up, and he could see that Claire was screaming at the police to release Mr. J.

The woman and child began to move toward Claire and embraced when they met. The little boy looked at the man in purple leg warmers and walked over to him. He stood over him and began to count. One, two, three, four and Alex gently moved the little boy from over the top of the metro man. The boy ran and grabbed his mother's' arm as he began to tear her away from Claire. Alex could hear him telling her *"Let's go get him. We may get to keep him this time."* Claire was left standing in the alley with an empty look on her face. She turned and started to walk back to the bakery. Claire walked by Alex as if he was invisible. She walked in the back door of the Bakery and slammed the door. Alex could hear her banging pots and pans as she screamed at the top of her lungs. He could not make out want she was screaming but it was very loud.

Alex realized he needed to get to the police station. He began to walk out of the alley, but he had a feeling he never experienced before. Alex could feel his body take over as he started to walk faster and faster. The Fedora was locked in his eyesight. Alex could not stop himself as his foot kicked the damn thing with all his might. The Fedora flew in the air, but Alex's eyes were still locked in on its flight pattern. Alex was out of control again because his body moved with such grace. His focus was totally on the hat. The hat began its descent and just before it hit the ground Alex's foot stamped the damn hat into the asphalt.

Alex had a feeling of euphoria during what seemed like a dream. It was a marvelous day with a happy ending. Alex looked back over his shoulder at the man with the purple leg warmers limp body sprawled out on the ground like a beaten fighter. Alex's mind immediately went to a vision of Mr. J. in a jail cell. Alex realized that he needed to check on Mr. J at the police station. He decided not to go back to Claire's Bakery when he saw all the store owners come out in the alley. They all came out and surrounded the man with purple leg warmers limp body lying in the alleyway. Alex realized that street justice was about to happen, so he decided to wait and maybe participate. He had already gotten his revenge for the time he was attacked in the elevator by the Metro Men's Gang.

Alex looked at the crowd of people. Claire who was leading the crowd as she looked at Alex and their eyes met. The moment was priceless because they did not need to exchange words. Claire suddenly left the angry crowd and walked toward Alex. When she got close to him, Alex said, "*I am off to get Mr. J out of Jail.*" Claire looked at him with a puzzled look. Claire asked Alex "*Are you stupid or something?*" Her statement caught Alex off guard. Claire said, "*Those idiot policemen always come to steal him from us.*"

Alex realized the police did not put handcuffs on him, and he knew their badge numbers, so he had to be familiar with them. Claire began to get angry as she explained to Alex. The police come and pick him up any chance they get. They pay him a dollar at the top of every hour to fix everything around the police station. Mr. J's Intelligence Quotient (IQ) has to be over 140. Mr. J is brilliant, he is near genius, but his social skills are in need of a major overhaul. Claire explained to Alex that there is something special about Mr. J. He has something in his heart that makes him extraordinary. Alex smiled and nodded his head in agreement. Claire stated they would bring him back tonight so he can sleep because he always makes it home to his alley every night.

Bruce busted out of his delivery shop door and screamed "*Its bath time!*" The mob all looked over at Claire, and she rushed back to her position with the mob huddled around the purple leg warmer man. Alex felt he did not have to help him because he kicked his butt. Bruce who was in a full sprint raised the bucket over his head and said, "*Make a hole.*" The angry mob made a hole and held up the same washing utensils that they used on Mr. J.

Bruce stopped and announced that they would not be using clean water. The water was from his private toilet. He added 1 liter of grease from Claire's bakery warmed to 50 degrees Fahrenheit for easy application. The mob cheered and began to chant *"Dump that greasy toilet water!"* Over and over until Bruce took two steps back, and with a leap and a bound dumped that greasy toilet water all over purple leg warmer man. The mob screamed in delight as they began to scrub that greasy toilet water all over his clothes and body. Alex could hear purple leg warmer man try to scream, but he was probably afraid to open his mouth entirely, so it sounded like a soft growl. Alex realized he could not watch anymore when he saw Bruce run back to his shop to make another bucket. Alex went to the street and hailed a cab so he could go home. He had another crazy day and needed to go back home to avoid any other shenanigans.

Chapter 8

There Are Exactly 9 Degrees Between Love And Hate

Alex woke up in the morning ready to go to work. He turned on the News, and there was a live report of a Homeless Man Claimed by a Family at the local police station. The story began to run over the television, and suddenly his cell phone began to ring. He dove across the couch and looked at the caller ID. It was Stella; he pushed to ignore to let the call go to voicemail. His phone rang again, and it was Amanda. He was tempted to answer but realized he wanted to see the story coming from the television. He turned off the cell phone and put it in his pocket. The cell phone ringing caused him to miss the majority of the television story that ran. Alex thought to himself, *"I need a DVR. I need to quit being so darn cheap."* Alex went over to his laptop, pointed and clicked his way to the Television Stations' website.

The front page of the website had "Leland Stanford Junior Local Transient Claimed!" They had his current picture, which was an unshaven, scruffy transient next to a clean-cut, dapper looking gentleman posted on the website. The article stated he is married to Valerie Sharp-Stanford with an 11-year-old son Leland III and three-year-old daughter Leila. There was a cute family photo with them standing in front of their house with a fire-engine red front door. Alex recognized the wife and son from behind the shops in the alley the day before while Mr. J. was being pilfered by the police. The article stated he would be in the hospital for a couple of days before they would release him. Alex figured he had at least the day to check on Mr. J. He decided to cut out of work early to ensure Mr. J. was fine and maybe handle his situation with Stella and Amanda.

Alex planned his day very carefully. He opened his calendar and checked Stella's schedule to ensure he could dodge her most of the time he was at work. He arranged his schedule to correspond with a later lunch. Stella does not like crowds, so he knew if he got past the late lunch he could leave early without seeing her. The plan would keep him one step ahead of the women's gossip network. Alex knew he would have to stop by the water cooler and ask someone to pull his finger to create a distraction. He found that activity always conjures up memories of the old and new Alex. There is constantly one person among the crowd willing to take a chance. Why not? The water-cooler area is an open space. The elevator is not.

Alex's workday zoomed by as planned. He was always two steps ahead of Stella. The women's gossip network was buzzing at full capacity. Alex knew this because the women who were siding with him would stop him and make small talk. The ones not on his side would give him the evil eye as he passed. The neutral women provided hand and eye signals to keep him from running into Stella. The late lunch went off without a hitch. He had several offers from women at the office wanting to join him. Alex politely declined and requested they schedule lunch for another day.

Alex worked for another hour but was worried that the water-cooler gossip would hurt his plans for the day. He could hear the people in the water-cooler area talking. That was good, but he could hear whispering, then loud outbursts of laughter. Alex knew something big was floating around the office, and he needed to disrupt the flow between the women's gossip network and the water cooler's open communication forum. He decided to test the water cooler topic of discussion by performing a necessary drive-by assessment.

Alex walked by observing the body language of the people involved in the conversation. They all stopped and watched him stroll by which was a direct indicator that he was the topic of discussion. Alex knew the pull my finger trick was not going to work. He made a beeline back to his desk to rethink his plan.

Alex sat for a few minutes to clear his mind. He knew what was needed to disrupt the communication channel that was building at the water cooler. The diversion was going to have to be universal and catchy. Alex thought about the advice Mr. J would give him in this situation. He pulled Mr. J's 20-dollar bill out of his pocket and waved it in the air. Alex cleared his desk, put up his files, put the 20-dollar bill back in his pocket and prepared to put his water-cooler plan into action.

He walked to the water cooler and stopped in front of Brad, who is considered the president of the Water Cooler Club. Alex leaned forward and said, *"I'm just a sweet transvestite, from Transsexual Transylvania."* Brad quickly responded with a loud and crisp *"Coming!"* That phrase prompted two of the women in the water-cooler area to say, *"Oh, slowly, slowly! It's too nice a job to rush."*

Alex faded into the background and then walked away from the water cooler gliding backwards like Michael Jackson in the smooth criminal video. When he got just out of range of the water cooler's area, he said in a high pitched voice, *"What interesting underclothes you have."* The people working close to the water cooler could barely hear him. Alex sat at his desk and waited for the outcome. The magical quotes from the Rocky Horror Picture Show were floating through the office. He successfully disrupted the Women's Gossip Network and the Water Cooler Talk Channel.

Now, it was time to make his break for the front door of the office. Alex filled in his timecard, called his supervisor to remind him he was leaving early and casually walked toward the front door. He made it to the front door quickly and made a sharp right turn toward the elevator. As he turned the corner Boom, he bumps into Stella. They collided with such force; he knocked all the folders out of her hands. Alex watched as the papers flew in slow motion hitting the floor in the hallway one by one. There had to be at least 25 folders with working papers in her arms. Alex and Stella's eyes met as Alex had not realized he was holding Stella in his arms. They were locked in an uncomfortable gaze. Alex and Stella were unable to utter a word.

Stella's facial expression changed as she pushed away from Alex's arms and bent over to pick up the papers. Alex thought about making a fast dash for the door but realized he needed to help Stella pick up the papers. They both awkwardly picked up each paper and stuffed them back into the folders. Stella turned her eyes away from Alex and quickly walked back into the office. Alex was standing in front of the office door speechless watching Stella stomp away. He watched as she walked down the hall until she disappeared around the first corner.

Alex's mind was replaying all the great times they had in the past. He remembered when she used to spend her time degrading his persona in the office. He was feeling confused by the feelings that were rushing through his mind and body. Alex placed his hands in his pockets and felt the same feelings from the night Amanda pushed him out of the door.

He suddenly was feeling as if he needed to take some time for himself and gain some perspective on what he wanted out of life. Alex's mouth dropped open as he remembered his mission for the day was to check on Mr. J. He turned and pressed the elevator button, so he could gain some closure with his friend, confidant, and source of entertainment. Alex reached into his pocket and pulled out the wad of cash. He pulled out two crisp 20 dollar bills and clutched them in his left hand. He walked into the elevator and pressed the first-floor button on the elevator console.

When the elevator began moving, he remembered his ordeal with the metro men. He started to giggle while he was thinking about how tuff the metrosexual men look dressed like a rainbow. Why was it so important to have great aromas come out of your butt? Alex realized he could be a weapon of mass destruction. He should bring world peace with his new-found abilities.

He was happy he was the only one on the elevator because as his urge began to grow. He remembered how Mr. J. had changed his life with his fluctuating concoction. Alex asked himself; what crazy man listens, pays money for a transient's advice and takes it. It worked, and now he is paying for it with 9 more floors to go?

Chapter 9

Who Let My Bum Out The Romp-Ah Room?

Alex found himself staring at the police precinct doors feeling relieved to be going in a place where justice always prevails. Well, at least on television it does. He pushed through the front doors, and surprisingly; it was nothing like on TV. The television precincts had people everywhere. The cops were interacting with common criminals, ladies of the night, families and general people in the main lobby. It was pretty quiet with a police officer sitting at the front desk looking at his computer screen. Alex walked up and introduced himself to the desk sergeant. He asked for information on Leland Stanford Jr.

The desk sergeant turned and glared at Alex with an intense look. Alex immediately felt a sense of fear as the desk sergeant inspected him with his steel blue eyes. The desk sergeant asked Alex to show two forms of identification. Alex froze as the feeling of fear began to grow inside his body. His eyes grew large, and he felt an impulse to leave the police station. The desk sergeant said, *"Son, I am not going to arrest you. I don't have all day so give me those two forms of ID."*

Alex reached into his pocket and pulled out the wad of cash. He held it out in front of the desk sergeant's face. The desk sergeant grabbed the wad of money; he opened up the first 20-dollar bill and said: *"You do not look like Andrew Jackson."* He gave Alex back his wad of money with a sarcastic smirk on his face. Alex smiled and pulled his wallet out of his back pocket and presented the desk sergeant with two forms of ID. The desk sergeant gave him a visitor's badge and told him to go see Officer John Griffon in room 341. He pointed to two large double doors and said, *"Son you get to pass go. Remember there is no get out of jail free cards in this game."*

Alex proceeded through the precinct to the double doors. He passed through the doors and to his amazement the area was pretty quiet. There were a few officers in their cubicles, but unlike on television, it was empty. Alex was looking around but felt a pair of eyeballs staring at him. Suddenly, Alex felt his back getting hot as if someone was staring at him. He turned around, and there was a short, stocky police officer in a black uniform walking towards him at a rapid pace.

He tried to read the officers' name tag but could not tell if it was Officer Griffon or not. He attempted to make eye contact with the officer, but the officer was focused on his direct path. Alex moved to the left so the officer could pass him. The officer stepped parallel with Alex as he began to walk at a quicker pace. He reached out and grabbed Alex by the arm and started to drag him towards the double doors. Alex panicked as he struggled to stay on his feet while the officer continued to pull him out of the front door, down the 10 stairs in front of the precinct, and down the street to the first crosswalk.

The officer let his arm go as he walked across the street, and Alex settled into a nice walking pace with the officer. Alex took a glance at his name tag and confirmed it was Officer Griffon. Officer Griffon came to a stop in front of a coffee shop. He turned and asked Alex would he like a cup of coffee. Alex reached over and grabbed Officer Griffon by the arm and dragged him into the coffee shop. Officer Griffon let out a laugh as Alex returned the favor by pulling him through the coffee shop straight to the booth in the middle of the coffee shop.

Alex released the officer's arm and gazed out of the front window of the coffee shop. The view from the booth was spectacular. The viewpoint was all-encompassing for which the whole neighborhood could be seen. Alex plopped into the booth seat looked up at Officer Griffon and told him I am going to have a coffee and a doughnut. You may want to skip the donut due to the public perception of police officers. Everyone knows doughnuts, crime, and violence is interrelated within the justice system. Officer Griffon cracked the biggest smile then he just scooted into the booth. He began to laugh so hard tears came pouring out of his eye sockets.

Alex looked at the officer laughing and let out a sigh of relief. He turned and began to gaze out the coffee shop window. Officer Griffon was still smiling but watched Alex looking out the window, and his laughter subsided. He was being calmed by the view from the coffee shop window. They were both looking at the view for hours, or so it seemed. The view was interrupted by the waitress who came to take their orders.

Alex never stopped looking out the window. He just put up his hand with the index finger pointing up and stated, *"One black coffee. One glazed doughnut please!"* The waitress looked over at Officer Griffon. He was at a loss for words. He just looked at her with a blank stare with his mouth open. The waitress looked at him and rolls her eyes. Alex looked at the waitress clearly not wanting to miss anything happening out the window. *"My Officer friend will go with the coffee, one lump of sugar and a jelly doughnut."*

Alex looks at Officer Griffon explains the jelly doughnuts are not associated with the law enforcement. They are associated with PVT Pile of the movie *"Full Metal Jacket"* so it is safe for you to have a jelly doughnut in public. Officer Griffon smiled, turned and began to look out the window again. Alex did the same for a few moments until he realized the waitress was still standing at the edge of the booth staring out the window too. Alex raised his hand, snapped his fingers, and pointed towards the kitchen counter. The waitress reached over slapped his hand down and left the end of the booth.

After the waitress delivered their orders Officer Griffon turned to Alex, pulled his badge off of his uniform and handed it to Alex. He asked Alex for an explanation of what happened to the purple leg warmer man after his buddies' stole Mr. J. Alex asked, *"Why do you want to know that piece of information."* Officer Griffon stated the precinct desk sergeant was showing a video of the day they borrowed Mr. J.

The Ignacio Iona Kniple, the man in the purple leg warmers, came into the front lobby looking like he wanted to report something. Looking at the video, it looked like he had been mud wrestling with a pack of cats. In the video, you could see everyone in the front lobby area covering their noses and fanning for fresh air. Ignacio just shrugged his shoulders and walked out the door with his head down. The desk sergeant said, *"The smell was unbearable, and they still have not gotten the smell out the front lobby area."*

Alex smiled with his full teeth showing. Officer Griffon's face became incredibly intense, as though he was anticipating Alex's response would be exciting. Alex said, *"Hold on! I thought this was about me seeing Mr. J."* Officer Griffon leaned forward and said *"It is, but I need to know why the crazy looking Metro Man Gang leader showed up at the precinct looking and smelling like the opposite of a true metro man. That is an oxymoron when you think about it. I gave you my badge, so it is, off the record."* Alex smiled and began to provide the off-duty officer the details of how the purple leg warmer man pissed off the bath mob in the alley. Alex did not tell him about his part in the ordeal because he felt it was a minor detail, and it would not make the story any more exciting. During the end of the story, Alex had the off-duty officer chanting the phrase "Dump that greasy toilet water! "Just like the bath mob.

Alex handed the off-duty officer back his badge and asked for Mr. J. The Officer raised his coffee cup in the air for a toast. Alex followed his lead, as Officer Griffon let him know he would take him to Mr. J after he finished his jelly doughnut.

The two men finished their doughnuts and coffee at the same time. They headed to the front door of the diner. Alex stopped the officer at the door and asked him to check his pockets, just in case he had a jelly doughnut stuffed in one of them. Officer Griffon told him *"That is not a jelly doughnut in my pocket. I am just happy to see you."* The two men smiled at each other. Officer Griffon reached over and snatched Alex by his belt and began to drag him out of the diner and down the street again.

Officer Griffon was dragging Alex down the sidewalk with such a speed Alex felt as if he was going to fall on his face. He was struggling to keep his footing. Alex could see the officer grab his radio and begin to talk while still dragging him down the street. They turned a corner, and there appeared a black-and-white police car. Two officers jumped out of the vehicle leaving the doors open. Officer Griffon pushed Alex into the passenger's door and said, *"Get in!"* Alex barely sat up in the passenger's seat when Officer Griffon jumped in and stepped on the gas. The two officers waved bye and began walking toward the precinct.

Officer Griffon was driving at a fast pace only using his flashing lights. He weaved through traffic quickly. They pulled up to the county hospital and stopped abruptly. Officer Griffon jumped out, and so did Alex. Another officer promptly jumped in the car and drove off. Officer Griffon began to walk into the hospital as Alex struggled to match his pace literally running behind him. It seemed like the officer was dragging him mentally instead of physically.

They entered the elevator, and Officer Griffon pushed the 13th-floor button. The doors closed, and the elevator began to move. Alex realized that his uncontrollable urge was starting.

Officer Griffon had a serious look on his face. He had his hand resting on his sidearm. Alex closed his eyes and squeezed his butt cheeks hoping to make it to the tenth floor without embarrassing himself in front of the Officer. The motion of the elevator was too strong as Alex could feel the gas moving through his intestinal tract.

Suddenly, he felt Officer Griffon punch him in the arm. Alex opened his eyes looked at officer Griffon with a look of panic. Officer Griffon put his hand out, made a fist, and put out his index finger. He said, *"Pull my finger."* Alex froze for a second, so Officer Griffon punched him in the arm and told him to pull his finger. Alex relaxed and let a long slow one go in the elevator. Officer Griffon reached over and punched him again. He let Alex know Mr. J. told him all about his little elevator problem. Officer Griffon let one go and said, *"I hate the smell of doughnuts, but mine can overpower yours with jelly."* Alex covered his nose and let him know that the scent was nowhere close to jelly.

The elevator doors opened, and they left the elevator in a hurry. Officer Griffon began to walk down the hospital floor hallway. When passing by the nurses' station, he greeted them by their first names. Alex could see a police officer at the end of the hall guarding a door. When the officer saw Officer Griffon, he moved aside and let both in the room. Alex saw Mr. J's wife and kids sitting watching television.

Mr. J was sitting on the bed with his eyes closed. Officer Griffon greeted Mr. J's wife and kids then asked how his treatments were going. She let him know he was about halfway done, and he should be done in about two days. Her eyes moved to Alex. She said you must be Alex. Alex smiled and shook his head yes.

She began to laugh so hard Officer Griffon had to keep her from falling on the floor. She said my husband has been telling me stories about how many times he saved you from what he calls *"Demons in the air."* He had me laughing so hard I almost postponed them regulating his medication so he could tell me more of the non-medicated version, which is subsequently much more colorful and funnier than it would be if his medications were correctly regulated.

She said, *"I hate to medicate him, but this is the only way to dumb down his massive IQ."* She stated even in his dumbed down state his IQ is still above 140, but he has a personality. If he is not regulated, then he has to free his mind so that his ass will follow. Alex and Officer Griffin looked at her with a dumbfounded look. Officer Griffin reached over and pressed the intercom for the nurses' station and said, "*Nurse Ratchet. Mrs. Stafford is cold. Would you bring her one of those jackets with the lovely white canvas, and the nice leather bound stainless steel buckles?*"

There was a long pause on the other end of the intercom. They could clearly hear the nurses at the nurses' station whispering. A voice came over the intercom, "*Please tell Mrs. Stafford; we issued the last of that model over two hours ago. If she is interested, we can provide her with a doctor's coat, a Billy club, handcuffs and a pistol from the police officer in REM sleep outside the door of the suite she is currently occupying.*"

Chapter 10

Can You Take Advice From A Recovering Genius?

Alex walked over to the bed next to his friend. Suddenly, Mr. J. sat up and began to scream at the top of his lungs. Everyone in the room was startled by his actions. Alex jumped backward and slammed into the wall across from the bed. Officer Griffon and Valerie seemed to be holding each other staring at Alex. Alex looked at Mr. J, and he was sitting straight up screaming at him pointing his finger at him. Alex again looked at the Officer and Valerie, but this time, they were holding each other with huge smirks on their faces. Alex focused on Mr. J and realized he was screaming pull my finger, Alex! Alex smiled as everyone in the room laughed including the police officer that was standing in the doorway.

Mr. J. laughed so hard he had tears rolling down his face. Alex realized the joke was on him, but it was worth it seeing Mr. J in good health. Alex walked over to Mr. J and gave him a big hug. Valerie and Officer Griffon began to make comments about Alex having a man crush on a poor helpless man laid up in the hospital. Officer Griffon said, *"Valerie, May, I take you down for a coffee so the two men can have a little male bonding."* Valerie accepted the offer but said, *"Leland, if you guys are going to bond use some protection."* Officer Griffon and Valerie walked out the door taking turns referencing cross-dressing and gender-bending movies. *Brokeback Mountain*, *Mrs. Doubtfire*, *White Chicks,* and *Big Momma's House* were just a few.

Alex took a step back from Mr. J once the room was clear. Mr. J was still a little crazy, but Alex could tell that he was very different. Alex asked Mr. J *"Do you remember the time you lived in this city."* Mr. J paused for a second and smiled. He explained he has had a small neurological problem since he was a young man. The difference is his need to take certain medications to help him control his condition as he ages.

Mr. J let him know he was proud of the way he changed his life. He was so tired of looking at a cool guy with low self-esteem. Never really finding a way to grasp the life he wants. Mr. J. said, *"All these years I have wanted to ask you to pull my finger, but my brain could not get it out of my mouth!"* Mr. J explained he enjoyed his time in his real non medicated condition. It helped him solve a few complex problems that will help people on a global scale. This would have been impossible for him to do in his current medicated condition.

Alex asked Mr. J if he had any advice since this is the last time I will be able to get it from the old Mr. J. Mr. J. said, *"Let me tell you how to get laid."* I see you have mastered the other romantic subjects. As Mr. J. opened his mouth the door burst open and Office Griffon and Valerie said, *"Oh No we just walked in during a Man Crush! Please stop!"* Mr. J. leaned forward and began to whisper in Alex's ear. Alex smiled reached into his pocket and gave Mr. J the two crisp twenty-dollar bills he had been holding for the last couple of days. Valerie reached over and snatched the two crispy bills out of Mr. J's hand. She said, *"Paid in full. My sweetie is a Man Crush money maker. This Man Crush pays quite a bit more than the cut-rate law enforcement people."* She stared down Officer Griffon and rolled her eyes.

Alex looked over at Valerie, and Officer Griffon smiled, grabbed the kid and hugged him. He slowly walked out the hospital room. He walked down the hall to the hospital elevator as fast as he could. He entered the elevator and turned around facing the hallway. Valerie and Officer Griffon came out the room and screamed *"The room is filled with the scent of Coffee and Donuts. There better not be a flavor shift getting ready to happen!"* Alex smiled and mouthed the words, *"Please go back and save the kids!"* He quickly covered his nose as the door to the elevator closed.

The is not the end…

The story will continue with…

The 9th Degree: Alex enjoys the fruits of his labor!

ABOUT THE AUTHOR

Being a creative person, writing is just a way of expressing thoughts that manifest themselves into art. Dealing with life's day to day situations provides an opportunity to shape the world into a happy and fun place. Humor is the best way to deal with the stress of today's issues that arise seeming all day. Time is the only commodity that cannot be altered, so use it wisely. Life is about enjoying the gifts and talents GOD has given us. Make the Heavenly Father proud by living **"The Best Life Possible."**

God, Spiritual family, People, Money, Stuff